Hug Time

• PATRICK McDONNELL •

LITTLE, BROWN AND COMPANY
New York • Boston

Also by Patrick McDonnell:
The Gift of Nothing
Art
Just Like Heaven

Text and Illustrations copyright © 2007 by Patrick McDonnell   Mutts © 2007 by Patrick McDonnell, distributed by King Features Syndicate   All rights reserved.

Little, Brown and Company ⋏ Hachette Book Group USA ⋏ 237 Park Avenue, New York, NY 10017 ⋏ Visit our Web site at www.lb-kids.com

Library of Congress Cataloging-in-Publication Data: McDonnell, Patrick. Hug time / Patrick McDonnell.— 1st ed.   p. cm.

Summary: Jules the kitten learns that giving a hug is the simplest but kindest gift of all.

ISBN-13: 978-0-316-11494-3 (hardcover)   ISBN-10: 0-316-11494-4 (hardcover)

[1. Hugging—Fiction. 2. Cats—Fiction. 3. Stories in rhyme.] I. Title.

PZ8.3.M459548Hug 2007   [E]—dc22   2006025289

First Edition: November 2007   10 9 8 7 6 5 4 3   PHX   Printed in China   Printed on recycled paper

There once was a kitten so filled with love
He wanted to give the whole world a hug.

"Hug the whole world, will that make it better?"

As Jules nodded yes, Doozy helped with his sweater.

There was no one this kitten wanted to miss,

So he made (and checked twice) a Hug To-Do List.

He hugged his best friends,
Mooch, Noodles, and Earl,

A butterfly, buttercups, a little gray squirrel.

He hugged all the birds he could find in the park.

So many to hug before it got dark!

Jules jumped on a boat and set out to sail

And soon he spotted a big blue tail . . .

Attached to a huggable BIG blue whale.

The boat docked in Africa and Jules kissed the ground—
The earth so precious, so fragile, so round.

He hugged an elephant

and a chimpanzee...

A giraffe,

a hippo,

a baobab tree.

Exploring the rain forest by foot and canoe,

Jules discovered a species brand-new.

Kneeling, he whispered, "We welcome you."

Off to India—with its tigers so few,
Finding one is hard to do.

He waited, he watched, he sat very still.
He said to himself, "I will, I will."

PURRn...

Traveling on, he hugged a gnu,

a panda,

a peacock,

a petite pudu.

A wallaby,

wombat,

and a humuhumu fish
(number three hundred six on his Hug To-Do List).

But at the North Pole, Jules sadly found
What it would be like with no one around.

So Jules was surprised when his tail got a tug

And a polar bear asked, "Would YOU like a hug?"

The world is so big . . .

And yet so small,

It's time that we embrace it all.

That's something that we all can do.

Start with the one who's closest to you.

PURR...

HUG TIME!